APR   2019

THE RUNAWAYS

THE RUN-AWAYS

ULF STARK

ILLUSTRATED BY KITTY CROWTHER

GECKO PRESS

I.

OUTSIDE THE HOSPITAL, maple leaves glowed red and gold. I watched them through the window and thought: It's strange how leaves are brightest the moment before they fall.

"Come and look," I said. "It's really pretty."

"I don't want to look," Grandpa thundered. "I'm not allowed out."

I was visiting him in hospital all by myself. I'd been there lots of times with Dad. So I knew how to get there. First you take the subway. Then you catch a red bus and get off when you see the church on the hill to your left.

It wasn't hard.

Dad didn't often want to go, because Grandpa was difficult. He always had been, but now he was worse than ever. He got angry and shouted. He spat out the pills that could make him nice and calm. And he yelled at the nurses.

"I'm shut in here like an animal!" he shouted. "What do you think I am? An ape?"

His face turned bright red and he swore, so Dad and I had to cover our ears. Dad thought I didn't need any more swear words than the ones I already knew.

I disagreed.

I liked it when Grandpa got angry. It made life a bit more exciting.

But it made Dad tired and sad. He felt awful seeing his strong, fat father lying there getting weaker and thinner. That's why he didn't like going to visit.

"Why can't he be like other people?" he sighed.

That was on Thursday. Dad came out of the dental surgery, hung his white coat on its special hook and padded around the house winding up the clocks. He always did that on Thursdays. There were nine of them. I followed him around.

"Can't we take Grandpa out of there?" I asked.

"No," said my father, winding up the grandfather clock in the dining room.

"Why can't he live in the old people's home here? Then we could see him every day."

We had a rest home next door to our house. On our street there were usually plenty of old people wandering around who didn't really know where they were. Grandpa could join them. Then he could come over to us for dinner. I could see him as much as I wanted.

"This isn't Grandpa's part of town. You know that."

"Well, he could live with us. He could sleep in my room."

"I said no," said Dad. "He can't walk upstairs. His heart's too big and weak. And he's too sick and angry and stubborn and crazy. You know what happened last time."

"That was just bad luck," I said.

"Bad luck?" Dad snorted. "He'd just had his broken leg pinned. Then he decides to have a go at lifting a great big rock and it breaks again. You call that bad luck?"

"I like him not being the same as other people," I said. "Shall we visit him on Saturday?"

"We'll see," said Dad.

I knew what that meant. When Saturday came around Dad would say that *unfortunately* he had too much to do.

He sat down in his special armchair, put on his headphones, looked at the ceiling and turned the music up loud enough to deafen any thoughts he had inside him.

"I'm going on Saturday in any case," I said. "I like Grandpa. And I don't want him to be lonely."

Dad nodded.

He hadn't heard a word.

2.

I USED FOOTBALL TRAINING as my excuse.

I asked for my weekly allowance. It would be enough for tickets. Then I packed my bag with the football socks, blue shorts and proper football boots I'd insisted on getting.

I had to think of everything.

"If you want something to eat, look in the fridge," said my mother.

"Thanks," I said.

I made one cheese sandwich and one with pickled herring.

That surprised her. "Have you started to like herrings?"

"No. It's for the salt," I said. "You sweat so much when you do training."

It was a shame Dad didn't hear that. He liked it when anyone was scientific. But he was fully occupied with the Saturday crossword puzzle.

When I was alone in the kitchen I took something to drink as well.

"It's lucky we decided not to go and see Grandpa, now that you have training," said Dad when I said goodbye.

"Yes, it is," I said.

I told them I'd be home a bit late because afterwards I was going with one of the football kids to work on our geometry homework, because I was worst in the class.

Dad looked up from his newspaper. "It's good that you're doing something useful instead of coming up with silly ideas." He smiled.

"Mmm," I said.

And off I went.

The silly ideas were waiting for me.

First I went a short way towards the football field because my mother was at the window waving, same as always. After a bit, I swung off towards the subway station.

I bought a ticket and when the train turned up I got on.

I could see my face in the train window, half see-through: a good ghost on a forbidden mission.

I got off at Slussen and switched to the red bus.

But before that, I lingered on the platform to look at what was, according to Dad, the city's most beautiful neon sign: a giant tube squeezing out a shining worm of toothpaste onto a yellow toothbrush.

It made me think of Dad. And Grandpa. And how different they were. Dad was long and thin.

He had sad eyes. Grandpa was short and round and seemed to have just one feeling in his body: crossness. When he was angry you could *hear* it. He smacked walls, stamped his feet and swore. But when Dad was in a bad mood he was silent. He'd go off by himself.

No wonder they didn't understand each other.

On the bus, I was still thinking about how different they were, while outside the window autumn shook past.

After a while, a big woman in a blue coat sat beside me. She smelled of sweat. I moved a bit closer to her. My clothes might absorb some of her sweaty smell as proof that I'd been at football practice.

She turned to me. "Have you got ants in your pants, young man?"

"No," I said. What was she thinking?

"And you're on the bus by yourself?" she went on.

"Yes, I'm going to visit Grandpa."

"That's nice," she said. "Will he come and meet you at the bus stop?"

"No, he's in the hospital."

"And your parents aren't with you?"

"No, Dad didn't have time. He has to do the crossword," I said.

She put her arm around my shoulder. That's good for sweat transfer, I thought. When she sighed it sounded like the bus doors opening.

"You must like your grandfather a lot," she said.

"Yes, I do." And I started to tell her about Grandpa. I don't know why. It was if my mouth was talking all on its own. I told her about the things we'd done together in our summer holidays. And how nice it was to go to sleep to the sound of his snoring. And how he was good at all sorts of things. Like digging up big rocks. And putting new tarpaper on the outhouse roof.

The more I talked, the younger and stronger he became.

"There doesn't seem to be too much wrong with your grandfather," said the woman.

"No," I said.

"He'll soon be back on his feet again."

"Yes," I said.

Then I started to think about Grandpa's big heart and his pinned-together leg and how Dad had said that it would never be right again.

Then we were at the church on the hill already.

I saw it through tears.

"Bye then," I said as I got off the bus.

"Goodbye," said the woman. "Tell your dear grandfather that there isn't a nicer grandson to be had."

"I will," I said.

3.

MY DEAR GRANDFATHER had just pushed the alarm button that dangled over his bed. He didn't stop pushing until the nurse came.

"What is it now?" she hissed.

She was irritated, and no wonder. Grandpa pushed the alarm button all the time. Because he was bored. To be naughty. Because he had nothing else to do. No holes to dig. No big rocks to roll. No roof to climb on so he could clean the chimney.

"Get a glass of juice and a bun for the boy," he ordered.

"No," said the nurse. "This isn't a cafe. And please

stop pushing the alarm unnecessarily. Otherwise I'll cut the cord."

"That's the most…" And he swore.

The nurse looked at me. "Have you ever thought about getting married?"

"I'm not sure," I said. "Probably."

"In that case, don't speak like him. Learn to speak nicely instead."

And off she went. I think she meant to slam the door behind her. But there was a thing on top that meant it could only close very slowly.

Once it had closed Grandpa pressed the alarm button again.

When the nurse put her head in he said: "You were right about what you said. Now you can take yourself off again!"

Before she disappeared I thought I saw a glimmer of a smile on her thin lips. It was good to see Grandpa still well enough to be bad.

"It's a shame about the juice and the bun," Grandpa muttered.

"It doesn't matter," I said. "I brought food and drinks with me."

I opened my bag and showed him the packet of sandwiches. A cheese sandwich for me and a pickled herring one for Grandpa.

He nodded. "That's not half bad," he said.

"No, and that's not all." I took out milk and the bottle of beer from the fridge at home that I'd hidden in one of my football socks.

"The beer's for you. You like beer, Grandpa."

"Yes, I do," he said.

I emptied water from the glass on his bedside table and poured in beer instead. Grandpa smacked his lips. And he put on his reading glasses so he could see the little bubbles rising. Then he took a teeny tiny mouthful of beer. And a teeny tiny mouthful of pickled herring sandwich.

That's not how he used to eat and drink. Normally he shoved food in like a bulldozer. But not here in hospital. Here he didn't want to eat anything at all.

"Ah," he said. "This is good stuff, this."

He had tears in his eyes from how good it was.

"I hate the food here," he said. "They've taken all the joy out of it. Not even the water tastes any good."

"Perhaps you should run away," I suggested.

"I did a lot of that when I was young," he said. "But I think it's a bit late now. Do your mother and father know you're here?"

"No, I ran away. I said I was going to football practice."

Grandpa's false teeth grinned happily.

"You're a clever monkey, Gottfried Junior," he said. "You take after me. And your running-away idea is worth thinking about. There are one or two

things I want to do. As long as it's not too far from here. Not with this leg."

Gottfried! No one else called me that. It was Grandpa's first name. And my middle name. I thought it sounded stupid. But when Grandpa called me that I liked it.

It made us a sort of pair.

We ate and drank, enjoying our sandwiches and drinks and the fact that we were so clever, both rebels, and we had the same name.

By the time I had to leave for the bus, we'd made a plan. Grandpa asked me to get his wallet, hidden in a sock in a shoe in the wardrobe.

"See you next Saturday," he said. "It'll be as much fun as…" And he swore.

The last thing I heard him say was: "Lingonberry jam."

I didn't understand.

4.

THIS WAS THE PLAN: I'd come to the hospital the next Saturday and there would be a taxi waiting outside. The money I'd got from Grandpa would pay for the car. I had to "for pity's sakes!" make sure Dad didn't come too. I had to think up a good reason to be away. Maybe overnight.

The last bit was the easiest.

When I got home I took my muddy football clothes out of the bag.

"Must you get so incredibly dirty?" my mother sighed when she saw them.

"That's what happens when you play football," I said.

I'd stopped at the empty football field between the old people's home and our house and rubbed mud into my clothes.

You have to think of everything.

"They have to be clean again by Saturday," I said. "Because my team's going away on a training camp. Overnight."

"Where?" she said.

"In Sollentuna," I said. "We're going to sleep in a school gym. We have to take something to eat. Can you make meatballs?"

"Of course."

Grandpa loved meatballs.

And my mother loved making them.

I suppose I was a clever monkey, as Grandpa said—a real lying machine. Even Dad seemed pleased. He was probably happy that I'd be away for the weekend.

He patted me on the head. "Then I'll wait till the

week after to visit Grandpa," he said. "I know how much you like coming with me."

"Thanks, that'd be great," I said.

So that just left the hardest bit to do.

Grandpa's idea was that we should run away to the house in the archipelago where he and Grandma had lived till she died, and where the next winter he'd fallen over and broken his leg.

And then he broke it again and ended up in a hospital bed.

"That's far enough to run away to," said Grandpa. "And besides, I have one or two things to attend to there."

"Promise not to climb up on the roof."

It was the sort of dangerous thing he often did.

"I promise," he said. "Listen carefully now. The boat leaves the jetty at Sollenkroka at one o'clock. Best if you're here with the taxi at half past eleven.

And it wouldn't hurt if someone phoned to say that I'm going to be picked up so they don't wonder about it."

"Who?"

"You can sort that out, my dear grandchild," said Grandpa.

I thought a lot about how it would work. I couldn't phone myself, not with my child's voice. It had to be someone who sounded grown up. And how could I order a taxi? I was too young. The taxi driver would ask to speak to my parents.

Then I thought of Adam.

His name was actually Ronny, but we called him Adam because he had such a big Adam's apple. It went up and down like an egg when he spoke. You couldn't help looking.

And his voice was deeper than Dad's.

He worked in the bakery next to the mechanic's. It was the perfect place for him. Bread and cars

were his big interests. Early in the morning he delivered bread to all the businesses around. And when he was free he went down to the mechanic's and helped out.

He was nice. He usually gave us kids stale buns. And if there weren't any stale ones he gave us fresh.

"Take this for the dog," he'd say, even if we didn't have one.

I went to the bakery and told him everything, exactly how it was.

Adam who was really Ronny stood with his arms crossed, listening with a serious look on his face, like a freckled angel in a white coat.

"So you want me to trick people?" he said. "You want me to call the hospital and pretend to be your father?"

"Yes," I said.

"And arrange a taxi and pretend I'm going to drive your football team to Sollentuna?"

"Yes."

"But actually, you're telling me I should help you and your grandfather run away?"

"Yes. I'll pay good money."

I showed him the money I'd got from Grandpa.

"Are you in your right mind?"

"Nope."

Then he took the money, shook my hand and laughed so hard his Adam's apple jumped up and down.

"Good as done, boy," he said. "I'm all for freedom. And I need the cash."

He asked where I lived. And for Dad's and Grandpa's first and last names. And the name of the hospital. And the ward Grandpa was staying in.

"You have to think of everything," he said.

"I know," I said.

He wrote everything down on a bread order list hanging on the wall beside the telephone.

"That's everything, then," he said. "See you Saturday at quarter to eleven. I'll toot three times outside your gate."

"Thanks," I said.

As I was on my way through the door he threw a new-baked bun after me. I flicked a hand from my pocket and caught it mid-air.

"For the dog," he said, giggling.

On the way home I chewed on the bun and tried to whistle between my teeth.

A flock of birds sailed past, high over the roofs of the houses. And I thought: soon we'll be on our way too.

5.

I WAS PACKED and ready by nine o'clock. I'd been allowed to borrow my father's suitcase. I'd packed my football clothes, an extra pair of underpants, my blue pyjamas, a towel, soap, toothbrush and a little tube of toothpaste Dad had been given as a sample from a toothpaste company.

My mother's meatballs were packed neatly in a special bag. There were a lot of them. She wanted the whole football team to have a taste.

I sat in the flowery armchair with my feet on the suitcase and the bag with meatballs beside me and I watched the clock on the wall.

I tried humming. It didn't sound any good.

"You're in a good mood," Dad said. "What are you thinking about?"

"About our team," I said. "We're going to learn penalty shots and dribbling and a whole lot more tricks. And when we go to bed we'll tell ghost stories."

"You should also be thinking about brushing your teeth after you've eaten," said Dad.

"Of course."

But I didn't. I thought how fantastic it felt to trick people.

I could get my parents to believe anything I said, even though I'd just made it up. No one could know what I was thinking.

I could do anything.

Like Adam, who was really called Ronny, I was "for freedom."

Was it wrong to lie when it made everyone happy?

"Would you play and sing for me?" I asked my mother.

"What, right now?"

"Yes, it sounds so super-lovely."

"If you say so." She smiled. "Just a little."

She sat at the black piano. Her voice quavered when she sang. The song was "Somewhere Over the Rainbow," about a country on top of a rainbow where everything is exactly the way you want it to be. My mother loved this song. She was still singing when the toots came. Three of them, as planned.

"Time to go." I got up.

"I'll help you with your bag," said Dad.

"You don't need to," I said.

"No, but still," he said.

I was afraid that Adam-Ronny would give us away. But he didn't. He stood outside the gate beside a newly washed van. He was wearing football socks and a cap to look authentic.

He threw the suitcase in the back. "Hop in," he said. "And we'll go and get the others."

Then he turned to Dad. "You should be proud. Your son really has talent. Especially for tricking the opposition."

"Is that right?" said Dad. "Good to hear."

He gave me a clumsy hug and some money in case there was anything good to buy in Sollentuna.

"Have fun," he said.

"I will."

"Will you call this evening?"

"I don't think I can," I said.

I sat beside Adam in the van. Now and then I watched his Adam's apple moving up and down. He chewed gum, beating time with his fingers on the wheel. He was wearing sunglasses even though it was cloudy.

He'd borrowed the van from the mechanic.

"Did you call the hospital and tell them we're picking Grandpa up?" I asked.

"Nah," he said. "I said we were going to pick up my father. I pretended to be your father. 'I see, doctor…that's good then, doctor,' they said. 'Nice for him to get out for a little while.' But it sounded more like it would be nice for them not to have him there for a little while."

"Yes, he can be difficult," I said. "Lucky you have a deep voice. But what will we do when we get there? They'll know you're not my father."

"I said that unfortunately I couldn't come myself. But that my son and his very nice cousin would come instead."

I didn't mind having Adam as a cousin, even if it was just for a day. He gave me some chewing gum. That's the sort of thing cousins do.

We sat in silence for a while, chewing, listening to the radio and watching autumn glide past outside.

Now and then I said something about Grandpa.

"You don't mind a bit of swearing?" I said.

"I think I can manage it," said Adam.

After a while I saw a shop. "Would you mind stopping for a minute?"

"What for?" Adam asked. "Do you want something to drink?"

"Yes. Can you buy a couple of bottles of beer?" I took out the money Dad had given me in case I wanted to buy something nice.

"No, you're too young," he said.

"It's not for me," I said. "It's for Grandpa."

So he stopped the van. He didn't want my money. He said I'd already given him too much. I waited while he went in and did the shopping.

After that it wasn't far to the hospital. It was where it should be, after the church on the hill.

Adam drove right up to the entrance.

He took off his sports cap and football socks and

put on another cap with a shiny brim, one like the ones the hearse drivers wear outside the chapel at the old people's home.

"Now let's go and get your grandfather."

"Try not to provoke him," I said.

6.

GRANDPA WAS ALL READY when we arrived. Freshly shaven, dressed in a dark suit, tie and coat. He looked like a child going to a birthday party, forced to put on best clothes that he didn't like wearing.

A pair of crutches leaned against the bed.

"There he is," said the nurse who'd followed us into the room.

Grandpa lit up when he saw me.

"Great to see you, Gottfried Junior," he said. "But who's this raving lunatic in the chauffeur's hat?" He nodded at Adam.

I thought: now the nurse will realize something's up. And she'll call Dad. Because the hospital was careful not to let patients out with unknown persons, that much I knew.

"Don't you recognize Adam?" I said quickly. "You know, my cousin. He's going to drive you because Dad couldn't come."

"Good afternoon, Grandpa," said Adam. He put two fingers to the brim of his cap.

"Don't be an idiot, nincompoop," said Grandpa. "How would I know you if you never come and visit?"

"And do you know why?" said Adam. "Because you're always so angry and difficult. Ma doesn't like it. She'd love to see more of you. But then you'd have to change and be like other people, she says."

I thought Grandpa would explode.

But he didn't.

He laughed. "Bravo, Adam!" he said. "You're not like the rest of the family. You're like me and Gottfried Junior. You aren't scared. Nurse, can you bring the pills so we can get out of here. My son, the dentist, is waiting for me."

Grandpa got his pills in two small canisters.

"The white ones are for the heart, the red ones help you keep calm and not swear so much," said the nurse, winking at us.

Grandpa put the canisters in his pocket.

"I'll get you a wheelchair," said the nurse.

"Like stink," he said. "I can walk by myself."

"No, you can't," she said.

She wheeled him out to the van. And we managed to get him into the front seat. Before we left the nurse stroked his cheek. "Look after yourself," she said. "Don't overdo it with your heart."

"I'll sit still and be fed the whole weekend." Grandpa giggled.

We didn't say much in the van. We were three master liars who'd managed to spring Grandpa free.

We laughed to ourselves at how clever we were.

The morning clouds had suddenly blown away. It was as if the gods wanted Grandpa to enjoy blue sky and sunshine that day.

Grandpa wound down the window and breathed in the fresh air.

"Ah." He closed his eyes.

Then he said "AHHH" again.

"Just say if you need to pee," said Adam.

"Thank you, but I'll wait till I get to the boat," he said.

He and Adam talked about boat engines. I know nothing about them, so I said nothing. But Grandpa had worked all his life as chief engineer on big ships. So he knew a lot about cylinders, pistons and things like that. Now he leaned forward and turned one ear to the engine. "It sounds like a screw's loose in the fuel pump," he said.

"I'll have a look when I'm back," said Adam.

When we reached the jetty Adam got out and took down the semaphore flag, so the boat would stop. We were the only ones waiting. We sat in the van till we saw the white boat steaming towards us.

"There she is, the terrible old tub," said Grandpa, wiping his eyes and blowing his nose.

It sounded like a trumpet fanfare.

We helped Grandpa out of the van. And we unloaded my suitcase, Grandpa's crutches, the bag of meatballs, the bag of things Adam had bought in the shop and another bag that was Adam's surprise.

"Cardamom buns, something sweet and a loaf of bread. I baked them last night," he said. "It's good to have provisions when you're on the run. I'll come and get you at 12 o'clock tomorrow."

"You're a cracker of a nephew," said Grandpa once we'd got him on board and Adam was about to go back on land.

"Grandson," said Adam. "Don't forget!"

7.

"DO YOU SEE THAT?" asked Grandpa.

He sat with his back to the orange metal door
of the engine room. I'd opened it a little, ignoring
the sign on it, just so he could listen to the sound
of the engines, feel the warmth from down below
and sniff the wonderful smell of oil.

He looked out the window at the islands we
were passing, at the cliffs rising from the sea, at the
pines and firs and autumn trees whose leaves were
super-glowing because it was such a special day.

He looked at everything he'd seen thousands of
times.

"Do you see?" he asked again.

"Yes," I said.

"You don't," he grumbled.

"Mmm," I said.

I understood that we didn't see the same things. He saw things that *had been*. The things he'd seen thousands of times when he came this way when Grandma was alive. He'd gone back in time. You could see it in his face. Even though it was just as old and wrinkly as always, there was a sort of younger Grandpa behind the wrinkles.

"What will we do when we get there?" I wondered.

"I just want to see the house one last time," he said. "I want us to light a fire in the stove. And then I want to sit by the window for a while and look out over the water the way *she* used to. I never quite knew what she saw."

"Maybe she was thinking about things," I said.

"Yes, but WHAT?" he yelled. He made a fist and I saw small red lines in the whites of his eyes.

"Would you like a calm-yourself-down pill?"
I asked.

"No, I wouldn't. I'd like a cardamom bun."

"I've got meatballs, too." I said.

"They can wait till we get there. Go off and buy
a cup of coffee and a lemonade, Gottfried Junior.
Quick march!"

Lemonade was Grandpa's name for soft drinks.

I bought a Fanta, orange as the engine room
door, in the boat cafe.

I drank it with a straw. Grandpa slurped his
coffee and said it was the best coffee he'd drunk for
ages. Then we ate one of Adam's nighttime buns.

"Why didn't you ask Dad if he'd come with you?"
I wondered.

"It's more fun to run away," Grandpa said.
"And he'd never understand."

"Probably not," I said.

"We're too different."

"Dad and me too," I said.

"We never understood one another. He didn't like nailing or digging. He was much happier with your grandmother. And she was happier with him. They talked and laughed together. While I'd go out and dig."

I thought about how often Grandpa had been outside, digging. "Can you love someone who's dead?" I asked.

Grandpa bit hard into his bun. "Time to shut your mouth, boy."

I knew what that meant. It meant yes, you can.

After a while Grandpa put his big wrinkly hand over mine. He kept it there till the boat had passed the white house on the cliff. The house he'd built with his own hands for him and Grandma.

He took up his crutches and stood on his spindly legs. Soon we'd head off. He stared up at the house.

"Do you see?" he asked.

And suddenly I did. I looked with Grandpa's eyes. There was Grandma on the balcony in her striped apron, waving her handkerchief like she always used to when we arrived in the boat.

"We'll be there soon," I said.

I didn't know how wrong I could be.

It took us a long time just to get from the boat jetty over to the gate with PRIVATE on it. Grandpa sort of swung along on the crutches. Every so often he had to stop for a breather. The worst bit was still to come. Up the stony path to the house.

"Please, Grandpa, can't I ask Matt to drive you the long way round on the flatbed motorbike?" I asked. "You can sit on the front tray."

"Not on your life," he puffed. "I'm not sitting on any devil's tray. I'll get up under my own steam."

"You swore," I said. "For punishment you have to take a pill."

He got one of the white ones. I was worried about his big heart. He swallowed the pill with a gulp of beer from one of the bottles I took from the bag. It gave him a nice surprise.

"Now it just remains to get up Rocky Mountain," he said.

That's what people in the village called it, the House on Rocky Mountain. Because it was so high up. Because the path was so steep and gravelly. And because it didn't look like any other house around.

It was as if Grandpa had wanted to build a castle for Grandma.

Beside the path he'd welded an iron railing. He took hold of it with one hand and put his crutches under the other arm.

"We'll knock this off in no time," he said.

It took two hours.

"It's these stupid trousers," he said when we arrived. "They're too tight."

8.

GRANDPA WAS ALLOWED to sit for a long while in a chair in the kitchen to get his breath back.

"Time for you to make yourself useful," he puffed.

I had nothing against that. There was wood, birch kindling and old newspapers in a box in the kitchen. I opened the vent, put in the wood and lit the fire on my first try. It didn't even smoke.

Then I ran down to the well and pumped up a bucket of water. I had to pump a long time because the water was completely brown at first.

When I came back Grandpa sat in front of the wood burner with the door open, looking in at the fire.

"Shall I call Dad and ask him to come and get us, Grandpa?" I said. "You look like you could do with a hospital bed."

I said that to rev him up a bit.

It worked. He got angry.

"I'll be dipped in duck muck if you call anyone! D'you hear me? Do you want to ruin everything?"

He shook his fist around like a sledgehammer. He was back to his old self.

I laughed with relief.

Grandpa looked at me. "Were you joking?"

"Yes."

"What a stupid joke."

"I just wanted to get you going a bit."

He smiled. He became chief engineer of all the world's ships again and started to bark out orders.

"Get the shovel and a bucket from the shed and dig up a few potatoes," he ordered. "You know where they are. Go, get a move on!"

"Shall do!"

Grandpa's potato patch, which he used to look after so carefully, was now completely overgrown. So I ran next door and dug there.

The tin bucket rang like a church bell when I shook it in front of Grandpa.

"Here," I said.

He said a bad word. "I never would have thought it."

"You swore again. That means you have to peel the potatoes."

He muttered, trying to sound cross. But he was only pretending. He rinsed and peeled and I put the potatoes on the stove to cook. Then I set the fire in the dining room. And I took out the meatballs to heat them in the frying pan.

I cut a few slices of bread from Adam's night loaf. And I set the table.

"We're almost ready," I said.

"Just one more thing." Grandpa tugged at his suit. "I can't eat in this. It doesn't feel right. It doesn't belong here."

He swore a long stream of words about his best clothes. He wriggled out of his jacket and waistcoat. And pulled off his trousers.

"Have a look for my old trousers in my wardrobe. Quick smart!"

"Now I know why the nurses are sick of you," I said. I tried to sound as sulky as I could. But we both knew I wasn't really. We were both pretending and enjoying it.

So there he sat at last, at one end of the dining table, as he always did. He'd hung his old felt hat on one of the carved lion heads on the back of the chair. He was wearing a stripy shirt with no collar, an old waistcoat and working trousers that took him a long time to put on.

In other words, he looked just like himself.

"Do start," I said.

Grandpa's eyes swept over the table to check that nothing was missing. I knew that look. The slices of bread were there. The butter, another present from Adam, was where it should be. The potatoes steamed in their pot. And the meatballs were waiting in their dish. The beer bottle was open. The forks were on the left and the knives were on the right.

Even Grandma was where she should be, because I'd put a photo of her as a young woman where she usually sat at the table.

I couldn't see anything missing.

"Lingonberry jam!" said Grandpa loudly.

"What?"

"There should be one jar left in the cellar. I've been thinking about it ever since I went to the hospital. Just run down and have a look, will you please, my boy."

What was wrong? Why had he asked me so nicely? It felt almost scary. I ran in any case, out and around the house to the cellar.

Grandpa was right.

On a shelf was a single jar. It said lingonberry jam on the label. Written in Grandma's writing.

When I brought it back, Grandpa stared a long time at the writing. Then he opened the lid and carefully took off the layer of paraffin wax with his knife.

"Go and get a teaspoon from the kitchen," he said.

"You mean a dessert spoon?"

"If I say teaspoon I mean teaspoon," he said.

When I'd served the meatballs and potatoes I stuck the teaspoon deep into the jar. I meant to take a good lot of jam on it. But Grandpa took the spoon from my hand and gave me a tiny little bit.

And he took almost the same amount himself.

"What is it?" I asked. "Can't I have more?"

"No," he said. "I want this jar to last the rest of my life. You can save your jam till last and have it as dessert. That's what I'm going to do."

He looked at the photo of Grandma.

Then he put his fat index finger into the mouth of the lion on the chair.

"Remember the time you painted these?"

How could I forget? Grandpa had been furious. I'd just turned seven and got a box of paints for my birthday. I painted the mouths of all the chair-lions blood red. I thought they looked good. Grandpa didn't. He took me by the ear and went around the dining table and pointed at every lion's mouth so I could see that none of the lions was the same.

"Do you remember what I said?"

"Yes, but say it again."

"I said that each lion was different because the person who made them wanted them to be.

He put time into them. Part of his life was in them. Even though he'd been dead for a long time, he was still here. It's the same with the lingonberry jam. Your grandma picked the berries, cleaned them, boiled them, put in just enough sugar to make them not too sweet and not too sour, stirred them and poured them into that jar. She gave it her time. And her thoughts. So part of her is still in it. D'you understand?"

"Maybe."

I didn't understand. But sort of. Enough to know that he thought Grandma was somehow in the jam.

I couldn't help smiling.

"What are you grinning at?"

"You didn't swear a single time when you talked about the jam.

"That was…" said Grandpa. And he swore.

After dinner he sat in Grandma's chair. The one by the window where she usually sat looking out to sea. Or whatever it was she was looking at. You could see the back of the section from there. The strawberry patch that didn't look like a strawberry patch any more. The white outhouse. And the cherry tree that had given me stomach ache every summer.

Now Grandpa sat there trying to see what she'd seen.

At least that's what he said.

"What do you see, then?" I asked.

"An old man in a felt hat," he sighed. "Hardly a lovable sight."

He sat there till the sun went down, red as lingonberry jam.

"Now we'll go to bed, runaway," he said once it had slid down the far side of the island.

"I'll get the crutches," I said.

9.

GRANDPA WAS GONE!

Last night I'd helped him, first to the outhouse and then to bed. He kept his clothes on because it was too hard to get them off him. When he'd gone to sleep, I sat up for a while and looked at the pictures in Grandma's Bible till I got sleepy.

I woke early because I needed to pee.

On the way out I looked into his room, the blue one, which once upon a time had been a ship's cabin. The blanket I'd put over him was on the floor. The crutches were gone. And the bed was empty.

As long as he hasn't tried to get to the outhouse, I thought.

That was how he broke his leg the first time. It was a night in February and minus twenty degrees. He hadn't bothered to dress warmly enough. Just put on his coat and stuck his feet in his slippers. On the way back he'd slipped on ice and had to crawl next door through snow and bang on the door to ask for help. Because he couldn't stand up to reach the door handle of his own house.

Why on earth had I run away with him? I was too young. What would I do if he fell again? He was too heavy for me.

I raced out as fast as I could. Hit my toe on the high sill. Swore. Opened the door. And there he was!

Somehow he'd managed to take a chair outside. He was sitting in it, staring out over the fjord, as if he was waiting for a big ship with throbbing engines to come and get him.

"Grandpa!" I called.

He woke up.

"Good morning, Gottfried Junior."

"You're an idiot," I said. "What if you'd fallen?"

"But I didn't," he said contentedly. "And if you think about *if* all the time you'll never get anything done."

"But what are you doing out here so early?"

"Breathing," he said. "And thinking."

"Thinking of what?"

"That it's time to clear the gutters," he said.

"Yes, but not today."

"No. We won't have time. We have a boat to catch. But could you bring me the clothes I was wearing when we came, some fuel from the shed, matches and the spade you used to dig the potatoes."

"What are you going to do?"

"Don't ask so many questions, just do as I say."

I did: I dug a hole in the lawn with the spade. I threw the clothes into the hole. I gave the matches

to Grandpa. And I poured a splash of fuel over the clothes.

"More!" said Grandpa.

He was back to being the chief engineer of all the world's ships.

"Go off to one side," he said.

He waited a bit till the clothes were soaked in fuel. Then he lit a match and threw it into the hole.

Flames whooshed up. His best suit burned fiercely. Black smoke rose into the sky, like a smoke signal from Rocky Mountain.

"Why?" I began.

But Grandpa put his finger to his lips. His eyes followed the trail of smoke towards a cloud that the morning sun had turned red. Not till the clothes were completely black did he turn to me.

He looked satisfied.

"Now we'll have breakfast," he said.

I fetched the garden table and put out a chair

for me. I'd made us each a sandwich with cold sliced potatoes and meatballs. I took them out on a tray with a glass of water, a glass of beer, Grandpa's pills, a teaspoon and the jar of lingonberry jam.

Grandpa took a spoonful. Then he put on the lid.

"Can't I have any?" I asked.

"No, unfortunately," he said. "You'll have to do without. I need it more. You know it was the thought of that jar that got me up the hill yesterday."

Smoke was still coming from the hole.

"Why did you burn the suit?" I asked.

"Because I never want to wear it again," he said. "Those were the clothes I wore to the funeral. Do you remember?"

"Yes."

Grandma's funeral. An organ played at the back. The minister had finished speaking. We were supposed to go to the coffin to say our last goodbyes. Grandpa went first. He stood with his hand on the coffin lid. "You…" he said. Then there wasn't any more. He went red in the face. He clenched his hand into a fist.

And he swore, loud and long.

Everyone squirmed in their seats. Even though I hadn't been to a funeral before I understood that this wasn't how you were meant to behave.

Dad had to go up and take him back to his place. He sat there with his hands over his face till it was time to leave.

Now Grandpa looked down at the hole.

"I wanted to say something beautiful," he said. "Some words about how much I liked her."

"She knew that anyway," I said.

"I'm not so sure. The nurse was right. I shouldn't swear so much."

"Just one more time," I said.

"What?"

"Swear!"

He did. And I gave him one of the white pills as punishment. Because now it was time to go down to the boat jetty. Down the long path to the sea.

"I hope it's quicker going down than up," I said.

"I'm not walking," said Grandpa. "You can go down to the village and get that bike you were talking about yesterday."

"I'll do that," I said.

But first I took out my football gear and muddied it like last time. As I said, you have to think of everything. Then I filled in the hole. Put the fuel can and the spade back in the shed. Closed the vent to the woodstove, and the oven, and turned off the power.

Grandpa sat on a chair and called out what I should do next.

"Good," he said when I was done. "Now you can look after yourself if you ever need to run away again."

The journey to the jetty was fun. Grandpa sat on the tray at the front of the bike in a chair we'd taken from the best room. Matt had tied it on with a rope so it wouldn't slide around.

Grandpa clung to the jar of lingonberry jam. He'd put the photo of Grandma in his coat pocket.

He looked at everything he'd seen so many times that he'd forgotten what it looked like.

When we arrived at the jetty his eyes were full of tears.

"The wind," said Grandpa, even though Matt had driven very slowly.

The boat wasn't due for a while. Matt put the armchair down on the jetty so Grandpa could sit comfortably.

"I'll get it later and take it up to the house," he said.

"You can keep it," said Grandpa. "I've finished sitting in it after today."

Then he sat himself up, turned his nose to the sea and said goodbye to the islands, the sky, the cliffs, the lighthouse and the eternally washing waves.

"D'you see the eagle?" He pointed with his crutch at a crow.

"Yes," I said.

10.

WHEN WE PASSED the house on the mountain I looked up at the balcony. But Grandma wasn't there waving.

She never liked it when we went away.

I leaned my head on Grandpa's shoulder and thought: It's not over yet!

I wondered for example what we'd say when we got to the hospital so that the nurses wouldn't ask how it'd been to have Grandpa at home, the next time Dad came visiting. Or say something like: So nice that Gottfried could spend the weekend with his son.

That would give away everything.

The whole thing was a great big bluff.

Grandpa would be in trouble because he should know better.

And I would almost certainly have to sit in the interrogation chair. That was the brown leather armchair in one corner of the living room. Dad usually sat in it when he was shaving. But if I'd done something *unthinkable* (that's what Dad called it) then I was placed in it.

I was perfectly sure that running away with Grandpa was unthinkable. I could already smell the leather of the chair.

"How could you do something so *incredibly unthinkable*?" my father would say.

Dad is a world master in unusual words. And that was a good thing because I learned a lot of new ones.

The bad ones from Grandpa. The big ones from Dad.

But had I really done something so incredibly unthinkable? I'd thought of others. I'd made Grandpa happy.

I'd helped him get to the old house he'd built one last time. He'd been able to breathe in the smell of the sea. And I'd been down to the cellar and collected the jar of lingonberry jam that he said somehow still had Grandma in it.

It was true that I'd lied. But if I hadn't, he would never have gone out. Not to sea. Not to his house. And he wouldn't have been able to burn his old suit. Because Dad wouldn't let him do any of that. He would have had to stay in his bed with the pillow behind his back being bored and pushing the alarm button just for something to do.

Now he sat and looked out through the window at the islands gliding past. And his cheeks weren't as grey as they'd been in the hospital room.

"Grandpa, is it a good thing to lie sometimes?"

"What did you say?"

He was still thinking about *his* things.

"Can it ever be good to lie?"

"Yes," he said after a while. "Sometimes lying is the only way to be completely truthful."

Then his face lit up and he let out a really terrible word. He looked pleased. "That wasn't badly said. Is there any beer left?"

"Yes, one," I said. "By the way, weren't you going to stop swearing? You could try doing like I do. Whenever I'm about to swear I stay quiet instead."

Grandpa drank his beer in small gulps because he knew it would be a while before he could have another. And he ate some more cardamom buns because the meatballs were finished.

He'd taken the photo of Grandma from his coat pocket and put it in front of him. It was so faded that she almost looked like a ghost.

"It's so hard to believe I won't ever see her again," he said.

"You can," I said. "In heaven."

"I don't know. I find it hard to believe in a life in heaven. How can you believe in something you've never seen?"

"I believe in crocodiles," I said.

Grandpa liked it when you were smart. He smiled so his teeth went crooked. He had to poke them back into place with his finger.

"Anyway, I hope not to have false teeth in the next life, if there is one," he said. "Or legs that break off at the slightest little thing."

"In heaven everyone is probably in top form," I said. "You and Grandma can fly around like a pair of butterflies."

Then Grandpa wrinkled his forehead.

"We're talking about how life is after death," he said. "Not something to joke about. You know, sometimes I dream about her at night. That she's sitting up on the cliff drinking coffee. Or hanging out the washing. Or anything. Then I wake up and I'm in that devil of a hospital." He swore a bit. "And I cry, even though I'm not a crying man. Because I still want to be in the dream."

I didn't take any notice of his swearing. Because it was appropriate.

"That's probably how it is there," I said. "Like in 'Somewhere Over the Rainbow'."

"Where?"

"In heaven," I said. "It's a song about a land where everything's just the way you want it to be."

"The only thing I want is for her to be there," sighed Grandpa. "Then I don't give a stuff about anything else. There's so much I want to do with her that I never did. And say that I never said. If heaven exists…and if I can get there, which is not completely certain."

"I think it is," I said. "But first you'll have to sit in the interrogation chair."

"What do you mean? What interrogation chair?"

"Oh, nothing," I said.

For the rest of the journey he sat in silence. Maybe he was thinking about everything he'd do and say if he only got a chance in Paradise.

Just before we got to the jetty he brightened. "I'll learn to speak nicely," he said. "I'll learn all those nice words. To be on the safe side. I'll do that for…"

A swear word was on its way. But he swallowed it with a grimace. Like when he drank a schnapps at Christmas time.

II.

RONNY-ADAM WAS WAITING for us at the jetty. He had his chauffeur cap on.

"Hi, old man," said Adam, clicking his heels.

"Hip-hip, young man," said Grandpa.

You could tell that they liked each other.

We helped fold Grandpa into the front seat. I stretched out in the back with the crutches for company and the bag under my head. It took a lot of energy to run away. I listened to the hum of traffic through the open window. And the brm-brmm of the engine.

Grandpa was humming too. "It's not rattling any more," he said.

"No, you were right about the screw," said Adam. "I sorted that. You should come and help in the workshop."

"I'd much rather..." You could feel the swear words on the tip of Grandpa's tongue. "Much more than going to the…hospital."

"Grandpa's given up swearing," I said.

"Is it hard to stop?" Adam wondered.

"It's possible…possibly," muttered Grandpa. "The…words just sneak out from habit. Best I shut up for a bit."

I poked him in the neck with a crutch.

"What?" he said. "Is shut up a swear word now too?"

"Borderline," said Adam.

Grandpa sighed.

I think he was actually pleased to sit quietly and think about what we'd done. And what he'd felt and seen. He wanted to keep it to himself. It was as if he'd put up a sign with PRIVATE on it, like on the gate to the house.

While Grandpa was being quiet I told Adam about our adventure. Sometimes he chuckled. Sometimes he clucked out a laugh.

"I'm proud to have your grandfather as my grandfather," he said. "Even if it was just for a few hours. And think how well it's all gone!"

"So far," I said.

"What do you mean?"

"At the hospital they think Grandpa's been with Dad. When Dad visits next time they'll definitely want to talk about it. And he'll find out we tricked them."

"Doesn't matter," said Grandpa, waking up.

"Yes, it does," I said. "Dad will be angry."

"Don't be such a coward, Gottfried Junior," said Grandpa. "I've had my best time in ages. And you've been able to enjoy my wonderful company for almost two whole days. Isn't that worth getting in a bit of trouble?"

"Maybe."

"There then."

But Grandpa didn't know what it was like when Dad got angry. He didn't shout like Grandpa. He didn't stamp his foot. Or make a fist in front of your nose. He tried to sound calm. But he wasn't. A vein would stick out on his forehead, and that was all you could see. And then he'd look at you in a way that said: "You're the one who's made me this sad." His rage could last for several days.

It gave me a stomach ache.

I wanted to avoid that.

"But what if Dad won't let us see each other any more," I said. "He might think we're not suitable for each other." Once he'd forbidden me to see a boy he thought unsuitable.

Grandpa looked uncertain.

"He wouldn't do that…" Grandpa paused, then he said, "Would he?"

"Maybe," I said.

"We'll have to think of something." Adam swung the van into the parking area and stopped in front of the hospital.

He went to fetch a wheelchair. Grandpa leaned back in his seat. He'd pushed his hat to the back of his head and turned his face to the sun. He closed his eyes and breathed in autumn.

He wanted to make the most of his last moments of freedom.

"Might be best to take something strengthening before we go in," he said. "You know what."

I took out the jar of lingonberry jam. And he produced a teaspoon he'd brought from the house in his pocket. He opened his mouth and I put in a small taste.

He kept his eyes closed while he swallowed.

"Medicine?" Adam came out with the wheelchair.

"Mmm, something along those lines," said Grandpa. "To keep me alive a bit longer."

"We're ready to go then," said Adam, when Grandpa was in the chair.

"Wait," said Grandpa. "Just till the medicine starts to work."

We waited till a nurse came out and asked what we were doing. It was the same nurse who'd wheeled him out when we left.

"So you've come back?" she said.

"Yes, I understand you've missed me," said Grandpa.

She wheeled him into his room. She sat him in the visitor's chair because he had to change back into hospital clothes before he could go to bed. She noticed his dirty working trousers.

"What have you been doing this weekend?"

"Climbing Rocky Mountain," said Grandpa.

"Yes, I can see that," she said. "And how did it go with your son?"

"He wasn't there," Adam said quickly.

My stomach went into a knot. As it always did when I was afraid. My mother was the same.

"What do you mean?" she said. "Where were you?"

"At home," said Grandpa. "That's where."

"Yes, at my mother's," said Adam. "He changed his mind on the way to my uncle's. He wanted to see her instead, because it was so long since he'd seen his daughter. He was so happy there, he stayed overnight. And it was the same for her. He didn't argue at all. And he almost didn't swear. He was completely abnormal."

The nurse looked very moved. "That sounds wonderful," she said.

"Mm, don't say anything to my uncle when he

comes in," said Adam. "Promise? He gets so cross when Grandpa would rather be with my mother."

"He's always been a mushy, jealous sort," said Grandpa.

"Promise, I won't say a word," she said.

She went to get a clean shirt for Grandpa. Grandpa and I agreed that Adam was a genius.

"My dear grandson, you're too good to be true," said Grandpa.

Before we left him, Grandpa put the photo of Grandma on the bedside table.

"Who is she?" asked Adam.

"My wife," said Grandpa. "Isn't she just so…" he paused "…beautiful."

I thought Grandma in the photo blinked a little in surprise at the missing swearword.

And Adam nodded. Because she was very pretty.

"There's just one more thing, Gottfried Junior," said Grandpa.

"What's that?"

He put on the face of the chief engineer of all the world's ships and said: "It's your job to make me learn to speak nicely before it's too late."

12.

ADAM TOOK OFF the chauffeur's hat and put on the football cap before he even started the van. Because my parents might come out to meet us when we arrived. My mother usually kept an eye on the street from behind the curtains. And, as Adam said, you have to think of everything.

I myself had several thoughts in my head at the same time. Firstly: how would Grandpa learn to speak nicely so he wouldn't forget when he got up there and met Grandma? And secondly: Did Paradise exist? And thirdly: What should I say about the non-existent football camp? This last one was the most urgent.

The lying never stopped.

You'd think of something clever. But immediately you'd have to make a new lie so the first one wouldn't be found out. And on it went till there was a whole world full of lies.

Lucky my mother had read to me so much when I was little that I'd become a master of making things up. Dad would be harder to convince. He was so particular about the Truth. I had to be prepared.

"Have you ever slept in a school gym?" I asked Adam.

He had, when he'd been on a table tennis tour a long time ago. I wanted to hear all about it. About the ghost stories they'd told in the evenings. About the smell of old sweat. How it felt to sleep on the gym mats on the floor. How they'd hidden each other's underwear when they were in the shower. And how one person got a fever and was sick in his sleeping bag.

Exactly what I needed. That last one. Dad would immediately tell me to open my mouth, look at my tongue, take out the thermometer and ask me how I was feeling.

"How did the competition go? I asked. "Did you win?"

"No," he said. "I got beaten almost immediately."

"That's good," I said.

"It was," he said. "Because then I could go to the bakery instead. That was where I found out I could be a baker."

"I didn't mean good in that way," I said. "I meant it's a good thing to say. If you say you're one of the worst, then people believe you. They believe that more than if you say that everything went well. Strange, isn't it?"

"Yes."

"And d'you know one more thing that's good?"

"No."

"They feel sorry for you," I said. "And that makes them nicer than normal. They tell you not to worry. And that it will almost certainly go better next time. And sometimes they give you something nice to eat to comfort you."

"You really can think things through," said Adam, impressed.

"Yeah, books are good," I said.

We were almost there.

The van swung in to my street and drove past the old people's chapel with the green roof. There was a hearse parked outside. I didn't look at it. I was thinking about what I'd say when I went inside.

I felt prepared. I just didn't know for what.

My parents came out the door as soon as we stopped.

"I'll be on my way," said Adam. "Good luck!"

He waved his football cap as he drove off.

My mother hugged me and my father took the suitcase that Adam had placed on the pavement, even though I said I could carry it myself.

"So, my boy, how's it been?" said Dad.

He was wearing the white patterned cardigan my mother had knitted for him, with his red Sunday tie. He seemed happy. He'd probably finished the crossword.

"I'm tired," I said. "I think I'll go and have a rest."

"Good idea," said Dad. "You can tell us all about it when we eat."

"Yes," I said.

I didn't even unpack.

I went straight upstairs to my room. I wanted to be alone. I lay on the bed. My room was blue. Almost the same blue as Grandpa's bedroom. Dark afternoon clouds were passing outside the window. They reminded me of the thick smoke from Grandpa's burned-up best suit.

I was really tired. And angry. I didn't know why. Maybe I'd caught it from Grandpa.

I dozed off and dreamed about a crow that turned into an eagle.

I slept until my mother woke me.

"Up and wash your hands," she said. "It's dinner time."

"What is it?" I asked.

"Rolled veal and potatoes."

I went to the bathroom, washed my hands, rinsed my mouth out and thought about what I would say.

I loved rolled veal with cream sauce. I poured sauce and mashed it into the potatoes. In the middle of the table was a jar of home-made lingonberry jam.

"Do you know that a little bit of your soul is in the lingonberry jam," I told her.

"What lunacy are you talking about?" said Dad.

"It's not lunacy," I said. "It's just how it is."

I wasn't completely convinced myself. But I wanted them to think about something other than where I'd been.

"I don't know where you get your stories from." Dad smiled because he was still happy. "Who told you something so outrageously idiotic?"

"Grandpa," I said.

Dad frowned. The corners of his mouth said he wasn't so happy now. He didn't want to talk about Grandpa.

"Enough of your imaginings. Tell us about the camp instead," he said. "Was it fun? What did you do?"

"Nothing," I said.

"You must have done something."

"No," I said.

"What are you saying?" said Dad.

"That I wasn't there. There was no camp."

"Really. Of course. So what have you been doing?"

"I ran away with Grandpa."

It was quiet for a moment. My father put in a half roll of veal and chewed so hard there were two round balls in his cheeks. My mother took some lingonberry jam on a fork and tasted it.

"We took the ferry from Sollenkroka and slept over in the house," I continued. "Grandma was there, waving from the balcony. You should have taken him there a long time ago. Didn't you understand how badly he wanted to go? You don't care about him. You won't even go and visit him in hospital."

The words streamed out of me. I didn't think about what I was saying. Or how I said it. It was Grandpa's anger that came out, and to be honest some of Grandpa's swear words too. I didn't want to lie. I wanted Dad to hear the truth. Then he could say what he liked.

My mother said, "Please."

I wasn't sure who she was speaking to.

Dad swallowed. The vein on his forehead throbbed. He frowned. I could hear him breathing in and out.

"You know what I think about lies," he said. "And you know what I think about swearing. We'll have to sit down and talk about this after dinner. Let us now eat in peace and quiet."

"I know how much you like rolled veal," said my mother.

It *was* the interrogation chair. Dad sat down opposite me so I could look him in the eyes.

I didn't. I looked at his eyebrows.

He didn't notice the difference.

"So then," he said. "This is a sad story. Did the dinner taste good?"

"No."

"No, it often doesn't when accompanied by lies. So you went with Grandpa out to the island?"

"Yes."

"And how did you get to the house from the jetty?"

"We walked up the hill. He didn't want to take the motorbike."

"How gullible do you think I am? Do you really think I'll believe any old thing you tell me?"

"No. But this is true."

"And Grandma was waving from the balcony?"

"Both of us saw her. It was her spirit waving."

Dad's ears turned red.

"That's enough!" he hissed. "I don't know what you're hoping to achieve by telling me you ran away with Grandpa!"

I didn't understand anything.

He thought that what I'd made up was true. And that I was lying when I told him the truth.

He had my suitcase with the football clothes in it. He emptied it out on the floor.

"These were clean when you left. Where would all this mud have come from if you didn't play football? And one more thing. I wasn't planning to tell you this, but Grandpa isn't going to last very much longer. His heart wouldn't cope with going up any kind of hill. He can't even go to the bathroom on his own."

"He can!"

"No. I spoke with the doctor last time we were at the hospital. He said that Grandpa's heart has worked all it can. It could stop at any time. So you can see yourself how unbelievable your story is."

Tears welled up in my eyes.

"I can see that you regret it," said Dad. "I hope you can stick to the truth in future. Can we agree on that?"

"Yes," I said.

But I had my fingers crossed.

"Good. Then let's leave it at that. Now can you tell me how it was at the camp?"

"One guy vomited in his sleeping bag," I said.

13.

I WAS WORRIED about Grandpa's heart. That it was too old, too big and too worn out. That it wouldn't cope with much more. That it could stop at any moment.

I was the one who'd suggested we run away. It was my fault that Grandpa had struggled up the never-ending hill. When he could hardly get out of bed.

And how could I teach him to speak nicely? So Grandma wouldn't be disappointed when they met in heaven, but instead her eyes would go wide and she'd say, "Goodness gracious, Gottfried, how beautifully you speak."

I spent the whole week worrying about all this.
The last hour on Friday I cried in school.

We were supposed to paint an autumn leaf. I made mine golden yellow and red. It looked like a big heart. And suddenly I started crying, so the teacher noticed.

"What is it?" she asked.

"I don't know," I said.

"Are you hurting anywhere?"

"Yes."

"Where, then?"

"In my stomach." I made a face.

What should I say? In my soul? Anyway, it was true: I *did* have pain in my stomach. My soul was like my mother's; it was in my stomach.

"Is something worrying you?" she asked.

"Yes," I said. "How do you learn to speak nicely?"

My classmates laughed. They thought I was joking.

"You don't need to worry about that," said the teacher. "Just try to find the right words. You learn with time. You have your whole life to do it."

That was just what I didn't have.

One of the pains made me groan.

"I think you'd better take yourself home and rest," said the teacher. "Drink a cup of warm milk. That often helps."

"Okay," I said, and I took my school bag and left.

I didn't go home, though. I went to the bakery. It was warm there and half dark, and it smelled so lovely it made you shiver.

Ronny-Adam had just taken a tray of cinnamon buns out of the oven.

"Howdy, my best cousin," he said. "Would you like a bun? And I could do with a coffee break."

We ate the freshly baked buns. Adam drank coffee that he poured from a thermos. I had a glass of milk. We sat on the warm tiled floor with our backs to the wall. It felt good to sit in the heat of the oven with your pretend cousin beside you to talk to.

"It was stupid, running away," I said.

"No, it wasn't," he said.

"It was. Grandpa's heart can't cope with things like that. Imagine if I'd made him die."

"Don't be an idiot, Gottfried Junior. He wanted to do it."

"Yeah. But I shouldn't have helped him."

"Rubbish. If his heart is on the way out then he knows that himself. He knows everything about engines. And the heart is a pump. If it was dangerous for him then he thought it was worth it. It doesn't suit a guy like him to lie in bed and stare at the ceiling. Am I right?"

He was.

Grandpa has always *done* things. He could never sit still.

"Yeah," I said. "And he got to collect the lingon-berry jam and the photo of Grandma."

"And he went to sea again."

It felt good to talk to Ronny-Adam. And warm buns were just as good for the stomach as warm milk. I was still sad. But I didn't feel so guilty.

One last thing was worrying me though.

"Dad and I are going to the hospital tomorrow," I said. "And I still don't know how Grandpa can learn to speak nicely before he gets to heaven."

"Words aren't my thing. Can't you ask your father?"

"No. But thanks anyway."

He gave me a bag of buns to take with me.

"For the dog," he said. "Say hello to Grandpa when you see him. Do you want to know the best word I know by the way?"

"Okay."

"Syzygy."

Syzygy. I hissed the word all the way home. It felt good in the mouth. Like *scissors* and *gee! Sizzle* and *jeepers.*

But was it a word for Grandpa? I had no idea what it meant. So I asked Dad.

"Syzygy, syzygy," he said. "It's great that you're interested in such an unusual word. D'you know what, let's look it up in the dictionary."

He went and got it, a blue book with gold letters on it. The dictionary he mostly used when he was solving the crossword.

"They're all in here!" he said with satisfaction, flipping through the pages. "Page after page of words in orderly columns. From A to Z. With explanations. Now let's see…"

He kept turning and then he pointed.

"Here," he said, reading aloud: *syzygy, a pair of connected or corresponding things.*

"Thanks, now I know," I said.

I didn't know what corresponding meant. But it didn't matter. I remembered the most important thing: where to find all the best words and what they meant.

"Is there anything else you wonder about?" asked Dad.

"No, that's it," I said.

I watched Dad put the book in the bookshelf. Then I took it and put it in my bag ready for going to Grandpa the next day. The dictionary, the buns from Adam, a notebook, a pen and the newspaper with Dad's crossword.

Grandpa was pleased when we arrived. He put in his false teeth and smiled.

"Look at this, here come the strangers," he said.

"How's Father feeling today?" said Dad.

"He's like a new person," said the nurse who'd followed us in. "He hasn't shouted at us, not even once. He only swears when he forgets himself. And he's even eating his dinner. I don't know what's got into him."

"I'm turning into an angel, sweetheart," said Grandpa.

"See?" said the nurse.

When she'd gone Dad asked Grandpa three more times how he was feeling. Because he didn't know what else to say. And each time Grandpa answered nicely that he felt better than in ages and that soon he would die. After a while Dad noticed the picture of Grandma on the bedside table.

"Where did the picture of Mother come from?" he asked.

"She came down Rocky Mountain to me." Grandpa smiled. "So now I have company."

Then Dad shook his head and asked one more time how he was feeling. And Grandpa said again that he was feeling good.

"Perhaps you'd like to go to the cafeteria and have a cup of coffee," said Grandpa. "You can buy me a treat from the kiosk on the way back. That'll give me time to talk to my dear grandson in peace and quiet."

"You don't eat that kind of thing," said Dad.

"You heard: I've become a new person."

"And I brought the crossword with me," I said. I took out the newspaper and gave it to Dad.

Grandpa blinked at me. We'd been thinking the same thing. We wanted to be alone. Dad looked relieved and off he went.

"I'll be back soon," he said.

But I knew he would be a while.

Grandpa sat up in bed with a pillow behind his back. He looked like a tired God leaning against a fluffy cloud.

"Now then," he said. "Have you figured out how I can learn to speak nicely?"

"Yes, wait and you'll see," I said.

I dug out the blue dictionary with the gold letters and placed it in his lap.

He turned it this way and that. "What do I do with this?" he asked.

"These are all the words and what they mean. You just look them up and put them together and then you can say anything you like."

Grandpa put on his reading glasses and opened the book. He ran his huge calloused hand over the pages. And sighed.

"There's a whole…lot of words. How will I do this? I'll run out of time…"

"You'll have to do your utmost, Grandpa. Think about Grandma. Best to start straight away."

We sat for an hour with the book in front of us. We got through half of the A words. Most of them Grandpa said he didn't care about. *Anaconda: a large, semiaquatic snake of the boa family*, for example.

"I've got no use for that one," he said.

He wrote a few in the notebook I'd brought with me: *Ambrosia: the food of the gods* could be good in case he was invited to dinner. *Ardent* because that's how he'd feel—"You can bet your lucky stars on it"—when he saw her again. And *amorous*.

"You never know," said Grandpa.

Then he'd had enough of words, so I took out the buns.

"You'll have to work on it by yourself once we've gone," I said. "You'd better hide the dictionary so Dad doesn't see it. It's his best one. But he already knows enough words. The buns are from Adam. He says hello."

"Say hello back." Grandpa put the book under his pillow.

Then we ate buns and drank water. Grandpa mixed his water with lingonberry jam. I wasn't allowed any. He drank *ardently* with small mouthfuls. "I take a teaspoon with every meal," he said. "It even makes the hospital food okay. And then I have one at night to give me beautiful dreams."

"You have to make it last," I said.

"I am," he said. "It has to last long enough to get me through that blessed book."

He'd just put away his jam and shaken off the crumbs when Dad came back, pleased because he'd finished the crossword, and holding a bag.

"Hope you like them," said Dad.

"I'm sure I will." Grandpa sneaked them to me.

"Unfortunately it's time for us to think about getting home," said Dad.

"Such is life," said Grandpa, settling himself into bed and closing his eyes. "Goodbye, my sweet little boys."

14.

GRANDPA GOT NICER and weaker with every week that passed. We went there on Saturdays, Dad and me. Dad sat in the visitor's chair for a minute or two. Then he went down to the cafe to do the crossword.

The nurse said that Grandpa had started calling her by Grandma's name or "my dearest one," asking her how she was, if there was anything he could do for her and saying how happy he was to see her because he'd missed her so "fervently."

"It's almost enough to make you fall in love with him," she smiled.

"I'm just trying things out," said Grandpa with satisfaction.

Dad thought he must have had a small stroke.

"Then I wish more of them had them," said the nurse.

Grandpa was different with Dad too. Much friendlier. Clapped him on the shoulder, even though he hardly could, and told him he knew he hadn't been a very good father. That he'd shown too little love.

"You were too different from me," he said. "You still are."

"Yes, luckily," said Dad.

"You're right about that," said Grandpa. "I'm pleased you're still the way you are."

It was almost as if they understood each other. Grandpa laid his great old hand over Dad's. They sat there a while. Then Dad got up and took the newspaper.

"Now, would you like any treats today?" he asked.

"Yes, if you wouldn't mind," said Grandpa.

Dad turned to me. "But none before dinner. And brush your teeth afterwards." He winked as he left.

Dad had noticed Grandpa's trick.

"He's not silly, my son, your father," said Grandpa.

"No," I said. "Just a bit hopeless sometimes."

Once Dad had left we played chess, just like we did on hopelessly rainy days in summer on the island. Grandpa won most times. But not today.

He lost three games in a row. He wasn't like the chief engineer of all the world's ships.

"What is it?" I said. "What are you thinking about?"

"What if I don't get to meet her. What if there's no heaven. That's what I'm thinking about."

"Mum thinks there is. And she's usually right."

"Even mothers can be wrong, Gottfried Junior."

I didn't know what to say.

"Only time will tell," I said.

Grandpa laughed.

"Yes, yes," he said. "But before we meet next time I want you to find out. Shall we play once more?"

He fell asleep in the middle of the fourth game.

I took the dictionary out of the wardrobe and put it in my bag because Grandpa said he didn't need it any more.

What was Grandpa asking, really?

How could I find out if heaven really existed? I was too young, didn't he know that?

At night I lay on my back in bed, looking at clouds through the bedroom window. I saw clouds float past. I saw the moon and all the stars that looked like the pearl sugar on Adam's buns. There were so many. And some of them didn't even exist. Dad had told me that. They were so far away that by the time their light reached us they had gone out a long time ago.

When I stared out into space I had a thought: if we can see things that don't exist, then there must be things that exist that we can't see.

I felt incredibly smart. But I knew that it wouldn't be enough for Grandpa. He wanted so badly to be sure. At breakfast I asked my mother.

"Do people go to heaven when they die?"

"I certainly believe that," she said.

"But how can we know?"

"You can't," said Dad. "And there's no point worrying about it. So far no one has come back from the dead to fill us in."

But he was wrong.

On Tuesday I found out.

My mother's magazine arrived: the one she subscribed to because it had such good recipes. It also had articles about people who'd experienced incredible things.

I read about a man who'd been dead for several

hours, but had come back to life. He talked about how it felt. How first he'd kind of twirled through a dark tunnel, then come to a place that was shining with light.

They even had a picture of what it looked like. There was a cliff, and a bit beyond that the glimmer of water sparkling in strong light from above. It looked like the picture at the end of Grandma's Bible where an angel stood on a mountaintop pointing to the land of eternity, and light was streaming from dark clouds like water from a shower.

Both were in black and white.

I took the magazine and ran in to Dad.

"Look here!" I called triumphantly, pointing. "Heaven exists, and here's the proof."

Dad glanced at the picture and the article. "That's just a drawing," he said.

"Of course it is. You can't take a camera there!"

Dad sighed. "You can't believe things in those kinds of magazines," he said. "They're full of humbug and nonsense."

"Mm," I said.

But I believed it anyway.

The person who drew the picture had drawn it exactly the way the man who came back to life told him to. "That's just what it looked like when I got there," he said in the article. I didn't worry about what Dad said, because he hardly believed in anything.

And now it was urgent. I didn't want Grandpa to wait any longer for me to bring him the happy news.

15.

RONNY-ADAM GAVE me a ride to the hospital the next day. He hung a sign on the bakery door that said BACK SOON. I'd skipped school after lunch saying I had to go to the dentist.

I'd cut out the article in the magazine and put it in my school book so it wouldn't get wrinkled.

When we arrived at Grandpa's ward the nurse said it wasn't really visiting hours. But that we were welcome anyway.

"He needs a bit of cheering up," she said. "I've done my best. But he's awfully tired and sleeps most of the time."

Grandpa opened his eyes at least when we came

into the room, and put in his false teeth.

"My little lads, just the ones I've been wanting to see," he said. He tried to sound normal. But his voice was hoarse and thinner. And his eyes had an odd glitter.

"Are you sad?" I asked.

"I don't know," he said. "The lingonberry jam's almost finished."

The jam jar was on the bedside table beside the photo of Grandma. There were only a few red drops left in the bottom.

"I know something to make you happy," I said.

"I'm sorry, lad, but I don't think I can manage any beer today."

"It's not beer."

"Is it buns?"

"No, not buns either," said Adam.

"What then?" Grandpa muttered as if he'd already lost interest.

"Heaven," I said.

I had to say it twice.

"You said I should find out if it existed or not."

"That was a joke," he said. "But I don't feel like joking any more."

"You can see it," I said. "Here!"

I took the picture out of the school book and passed him his reading glasses that were on the notebook where he'd written all the words he wanted to learn.

"I'm not in the mood for jokes," said Grandpa.

I said it wasn't a joke. That this was really how it was. That someone who'd been dead had told it to the person who did the drawing.

Grandpa sighed and was about to give me back the picture when his face lit up. As if it was lit up by the light shining in the picture. He looked at it and smiled. There were tears in his eyes. His mouth moved, even though no sound came.

That lasted for about a minute. Then he woke up again.

"Did you see her?" he said.

"No," said Adam.

"See who?" I asked.

"You know who," said Grandpa.

He said that Grandma had come out and stood behind one of the cliffs. She was wearing her usual old stripy apron. And a shawl over her head. She didn't say anything. Just looked at him and seemed sort of amused.

"You know how she could look, Gottfried Junior?"

"Yes."

"That's how she was."

Adam looked doubtful. Although he didn't want to say anything because Grandpa seemed so pleased. But Grandpa saw his hesitation.

"You think it was a dream, don't you."

"I don't know," said Adam, carefully.

"It probably was in a way," said Grandpa. "Because she only showed herself to me. She appeared like a vision. How else could she do it?"

"Yeah, that's true," said Adam.

After a while Adam said goodbye to Grandpa. He even gave him a hug, even though Grandpa wasn't the kind of person you hug.

"I'll go and wait in the car," he said. "So you can be by yourselves for a bit."

I sat still beside the bed.

I held Grandpa's hand. After a while he went to sleep. I looked at him and thought about all the things we'd done together. He looked happy.

He snored quietly.

It sounded like a ship starting its engines, about to depart.

ON FRIDAY AS I WALKED home from school I saw a crow flying higher and higher into space, until it turned into an eagle.

Grandpa had run away again.

This time he wasn't coming back.